By The Light of The Halloween Moon

by Caroline Stutson
illustrated by Kevin Hawkes

Marshall Cavendish Children

Text copyright © 1993 by Caroline Stutson
Illustrations copyright © 1993 by Kevin Hawkes

First published in 1993 by Lothrop, Lee, & Shepard Books

All rights reserved
Marshall Cavendish Corporation, 99 White Plains Road, Tarrytown, NY 10591
www.marshallcavendish.us/kids

Library of Congress Cataloging-in-Publication Data
Stutson, Caroline.
  By the light of the Halloween moon / by Caroline Stutson ; illustrated by Kevin Hawkes. — 1st ed.
    p. cm.
  Summary: In this cumulative tale, a host of Halloween spooks, including a cat, a witch, and a ghoul,
are drawn to the tapping of a little girl's toe.
  ISBN 978-0-7614-5553-0
  [1. Halloween—Fiction. 2. Stories in rhyme.] I. Hawkes, Kevin, ill. II. Title.
  PZ8.3.S925By 2009
  [E]—dc22
                      2008022965

Printed in Malaysia
First Marshall Cavendish edition, 2009
1 3 5 6 4 2

mc Marshall Cavendish
Children

For Al and Alec! — C.S.
For Susan Pearson — K.H.

A toe!
A lean and gleaming toe
That taps a tune in the dead of night
By the light, by the light,
By the silvery light of the Halloween moon!

A cat!
A thin black wisp of a spying cat
Who eyes the toe
That taps a tune in the dead of night
By the light, by the light,
By the silvery light of the Halloween moon!

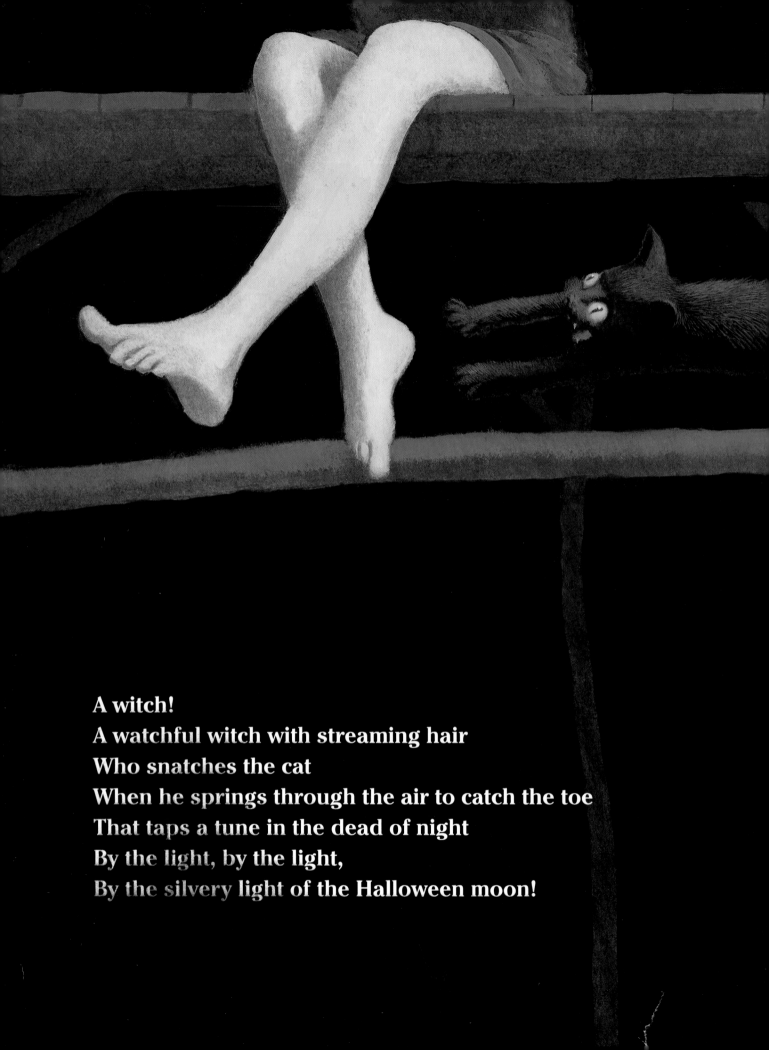

A witch!
A watchful witch with streaming hair
Who snatches the cat
When he springs through the air to catch the toe
That taps a tune in the dead of night
By the light, by the light,
By the silvery light of the Halloween moon!

A bat!
A bungling bouncy breezy bat

Who bumps the witch as she snatches the cat
When he springs through the air to catch the toe
That taps a tune in the dead of night
By the light, by the light,
By the silvery light of the Halloween moon!

A ghoul!
A ghastly drooling graveyard ghoul

Who swats at the bat
Who bumps the witch as she snatches the cat
When he springs through the air to catch the toe
That taps a tune in the dead of night
By the light, by the light,
By the silvery light of the Halloween moon!

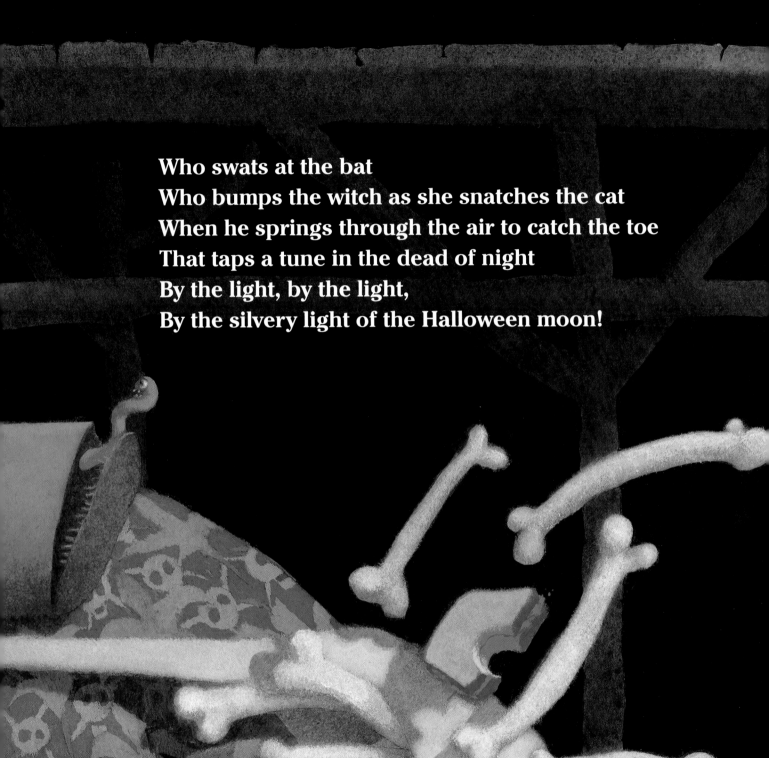

A ghost!
A williwaw ghost

Who trips the ghoul
Who swats at the bat
Who bumps the witch as she snatches the cat
When he springs through the air to catch the toe
That taps a tune in the dead of night
By the light, by the light,
By the silvery light of the Halloween moon!

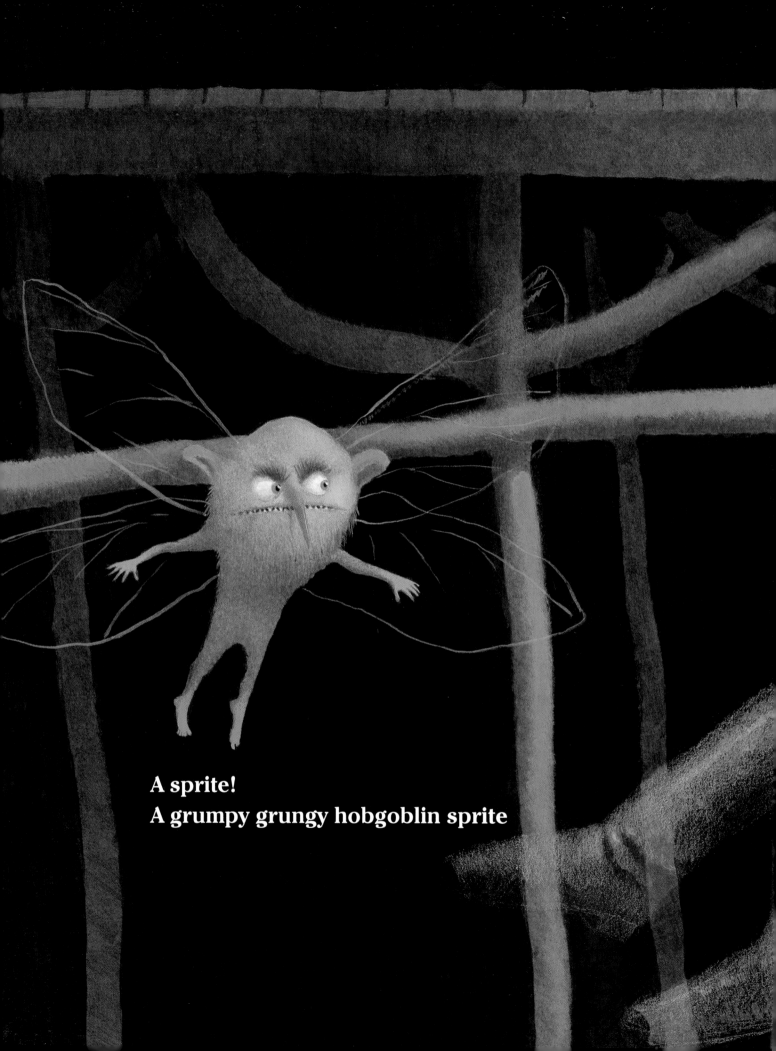

A sprite!
A grumpy grungy hobgoblin sprite

Who bites the ghost
Who trips the ghoul
Who swats at the bat
Who bumps the witch as she snatches the cat
When he springs through the air to catch the toe
That taps a tune in the dead of night
By the light, by the light
By the silvery light of the Halloween moon!

A girl!
A small bright slip of a smiling girl

Who smacks the sprite
Who bites the ghost
Who trips the ghoul
Who swats at the bat
Who bumps the witch as she snatches the cat
When he springs through the air to catch the toe
That taps a tune in the dead of night

By the light, by the light,
By the silvery light of the Halloween moon!